DISNEP · PIXAR

THE INCREDIBLES

A SUPER FRIEND

ADVANCE
PUBLISHERS

Frozone was the coolest Super of all. In fact, he was so cool he could freeze the moisture in the air to make ice and snow. And when he needed to move fast, he skated or snowboarded on the ice he had made. Frozone was agile, speedy, and quick thinking, but most important—when the action got hot, Frozone never lost his cool!

Frozone was Mr. Incredible's best friend and the best man at his wedding to Elastigirl. The two buddies had fought evil and stopped disasters hundreds of times together. Even when they were going by their secret identities as Lucius Best and Bob Parr they watched out for each other.

With his hip attitude and style, Lucius Best, aka Frozone, knows the meaning of the phrase "chill out." The coolest superhero on the planet, he is able to freeze water and moisture in the air, and throw out walls, sheets, chutes, and whole ski runs of snow and ice.

When the government forced all Supers into a Super Relocation Program and told them they could no longer use their powers, Frozone and Bob stuck together.

But there was one big difference between them: Frozone chilled out about not using his super powers, Bob didn't. He was miserable. Frozone realized that Bob's unhappiness stressed out his wife, Helen, and his kids, Dash and Violet. So because he was Bob's best friend, Frozone tried to cheer him up— even if it meant doing things Frozone didn't *really* want to do.

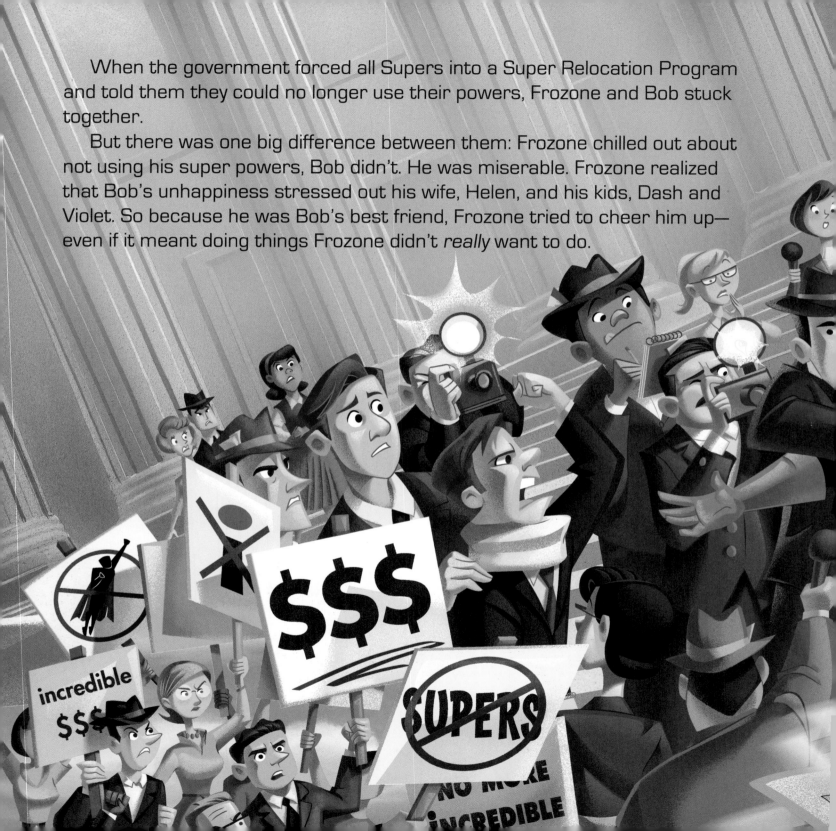

incredible
$$$

$$$

SUPERS

NO MORE
INCREDIBLE

In his heyday,
Mr. Incredible's
rugged good looks,
easy charm, and,
of course, his
megastrength made
him the most popular
Super by far. Loved
by the public, many
statues were made
in his honor,
and he received
numerous awards.

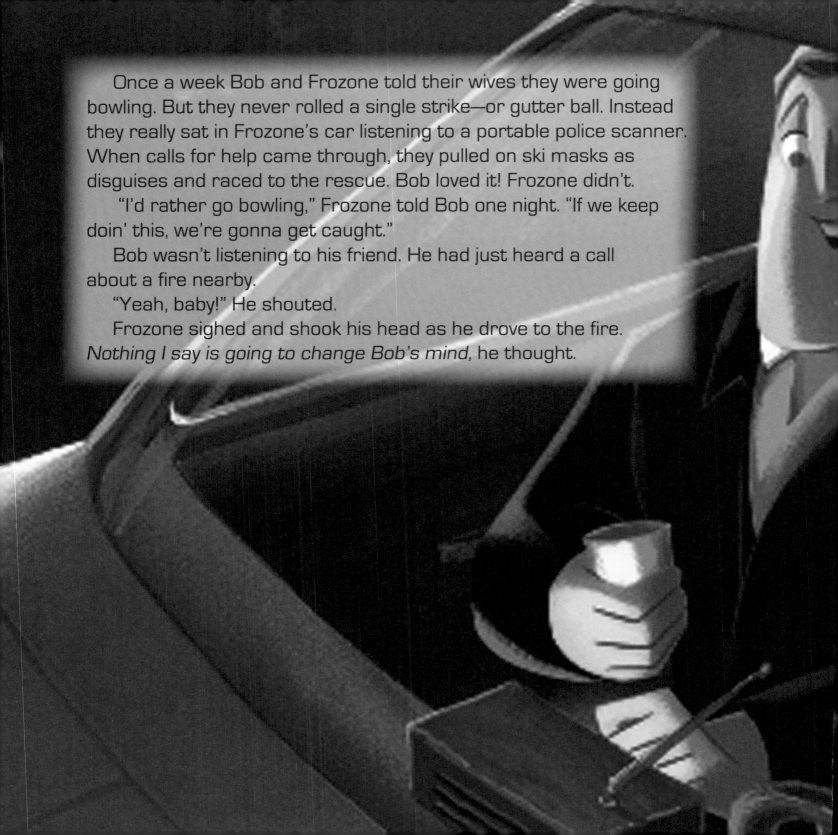

Once a week Bob and Frozone told their wives they were going bowling. But they never rolled a single strike—or gutter ball. Instead they really sat in Frozone's car listening to a portable police scanner. When calls for help came through, they pulled on ski masks as disguises and raced to the rescue. Bob loved it! Frozone didn't.

"I'd rather go bowling," Frozone told Bob one night. "If we keep doin' this, we're gonna get caught."

Bob wasn't listening to his friend. He had just heard a call about a fire nearby.

"Yeah, baby!" He shouted.

Frozone sighed and shook his head as he drove to the fire. *Nothing I say is going to change Bob's mind,* he thought.

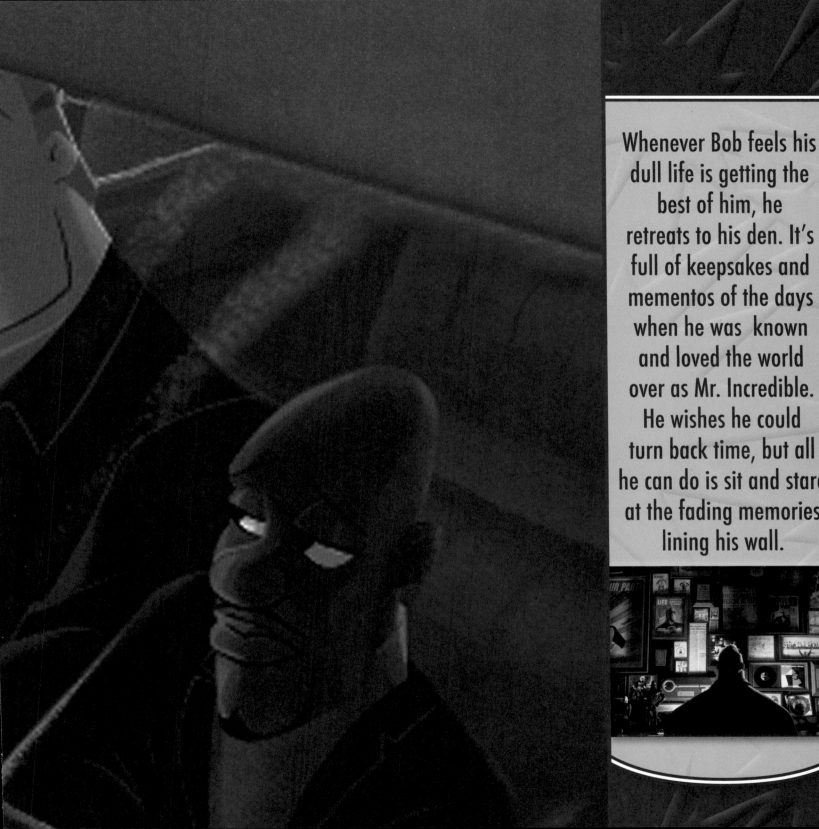

Whenever Bob feels his dull life is getting the best of him, he retreats to his den. It's full of keepsakes and mementos of the days when he was known and loved the world over as Mr. Incredible. He wishes he could turn back time, but all he can do is sit and stare at the fading memories lining his wall.

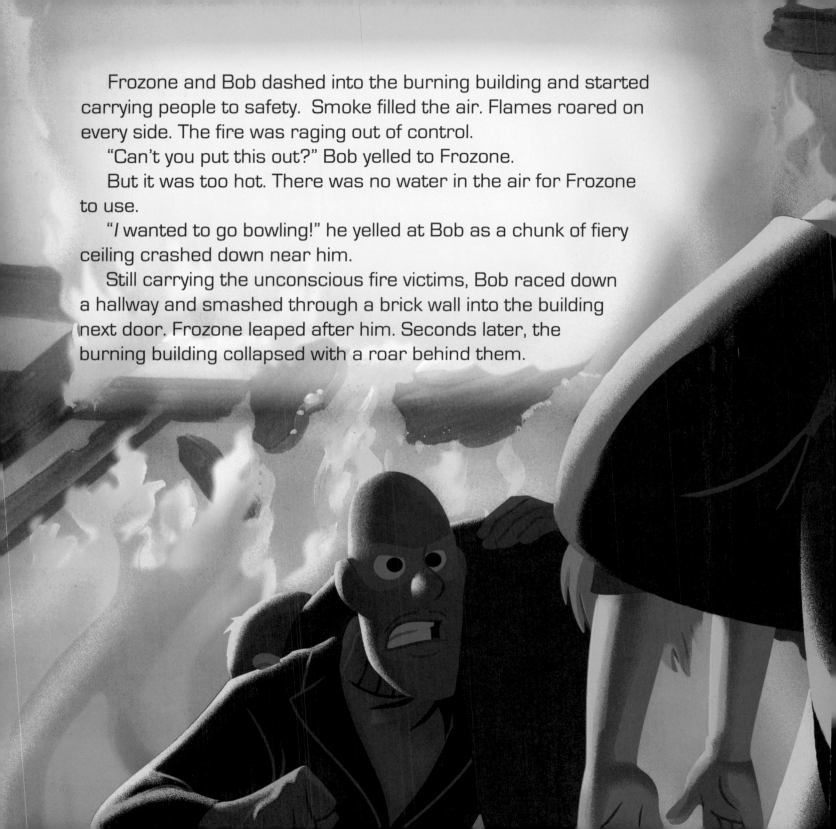

Frozone and Bob dashed into the burning building and started carrying people to safety. Smoke filled the air. Flames roared on every side. The fire was raging out of control.

"Can't you put this out?" Bob yelled to Frozone.

But it was too hot. There was no water in the air for Frozone to use.

"*I* wanted to go bowling!" he yelled at Bob as a chunk of fiery ceiling crashed down near him.

Still carrying the unconscious fire victims, Bob raced down a hallway and smashed through a brick wall into the building next door. Frozone leaped after him. Seconds later, the burning building collapsed with a roar behind them.

When Bob is late coming home from bowling with his friend (and fellow Super) Lucius, Helen waits up for him. She spots a piece of rubble on Bob's shoulder and is horrified to discover that the pair didn't go bowling at all—in fact, they accidentally knocked down a building.

Suddenly, they heard alarms blaring.

"Oh no!" Frozone yelled, looking around. They had crashed into a jewelry store. In their ski masks, they looked like burglars. Just then, a policeman raced into the store with his pistol drawn.

"Freeze!" he yelled.

Frozone edged toward the water cooler.

"I'm thirsty. I'm just getting a drink," he said. He sipped a cup of water slowly. Then he raised his hands and a frigid blast split the air. Suddenly, the policeman was encased in solid ice. Frozone and Bob got away—barely.

"That was way too close," Frozone said. "We are not doing that again."

Bob didn't agree. He wanted to keep helping people, even if the government said he wasn't supposed to use his powers.

But Frozone had had enough. Bob is on his own, he thought. Even if he is my best friend.

Frozone can freeze people in their tracks without harming them— just as he did to this rookie policeman who mistakes the pair for criminals. And before the law can thaw, Bob and Frozone are gone!

Frozone didn't notice the mysterious woman watching from a car parked nearby. And Bob didn't tell him about her mysterious message or his top secret mission to Nomanisan Island to destroy a deadly robot called the Omnidroid 9000.

But when Bob started getting in shape again, Frozone wondered what his friend was up to. He called Helen to find out, but she was gone. So were Dash and Violet.

Frozone tried to stay cool, but he was worried. Are Bob and his family okay? he wondered. What is going on?

He soon found out.

The mysterious message was from a woman named Mirage who said she is from a top secret government division.

It is up to Mr. Incredible to stop an unruly robot at a remote testing facility on the island of Nomanisan. The same robot that is out of control and threatening to destroy millions of dollars' worth of research.

The next evening, Frozone dressed in his coolest clothes for a dinner date with his wife, Honey. Suddenly loud booms shook the apartment. Frozone looked outside and saw the Omindroid crashing through the city streets.

Someone needs to stop that monster! Frozone thought. Then he realized that the someone was *him*. As far as he knew, he was the only Super around. Bob was right, Frozone thought. *I have to use my powers. Helping people is what they're for.*

"Honey!" he called to his wife. "Where's my Super suit?"

"Don't you think about running off and doing no derring-do," Honey replied. "We've been planning this dinner for two months!"

"The public is in danger. We are talking about the greater good!" Frozone answered.

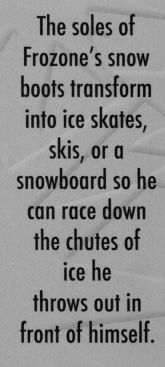

The soles of Frozone's snow boots transform into ice skates, skis, or a snowboard so he can race down the chutes of ice he throws out in front of himself.

Frozone pulled on his suit and helmet and raced down an ice ramp into the street. To his surprise, Bob and the entire Incredible family were already there. They were battling the Omnidroid—and they needed his help!

Frozone threw massive chunks of ice to freeze the Omnidroid's claws, but the powerful robot shook it off. Dash raced past with the remote that controlled the Omnidroid, and the vicious robot started after him. Instantly, Frozone created an icy path, skated to Dash, and scooped him up. Skating so fast his arms and legs blurred, Frozone carried Dash back to his family.

But the Omnidroid was rumbling toward them.

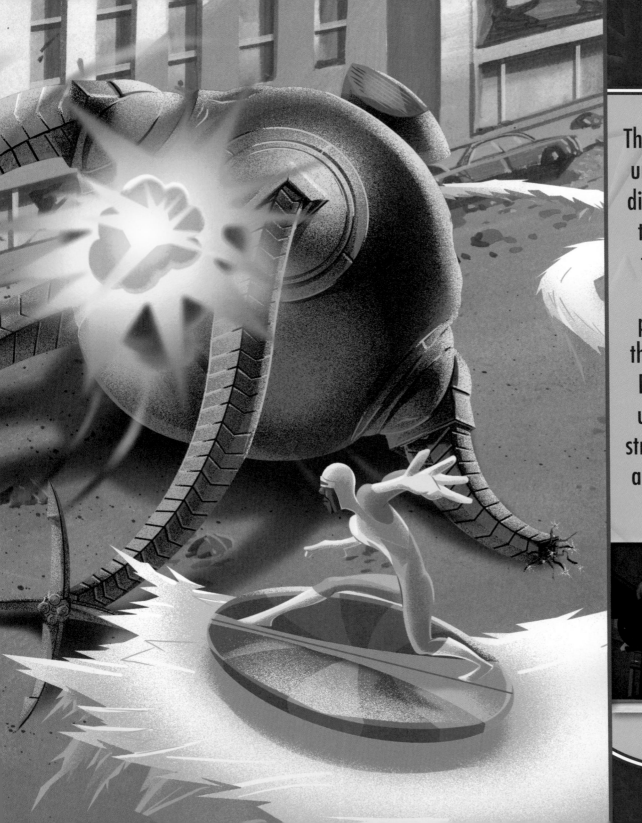

The Omnidroid seemed unstoppable. Frozone did what he could, but to defeat this robot, the Incredibles had to bring all their powers into play. As the Omnidroid shot at Dash, Helen yanked up a manhole cover, stretched her arms out, and hammered at the robot's gun turret.

I can't outrace this robot, Frozone thought. *I have to think of another way to stop it!*

He threw a sheet of ice onto the street. The Omnidroid slipped and fell. A claw broke off, but the Omnidroid kept coming. Bob grabbed the broken claw and pointed it at the advancing machine.

"Buy us some time," he shouted to Frozone.

Frozone nodded and raced in front of the Omnidroid sending up ice walls as thick as buildings in front of it. The Omnidroid crashed through them as though they were paper. Again and again Frozone threw up ice walls. Again and again the robot smashed them down. But Frozone was slowing it down.

"Everybody out of the way!" Bob shouted.
Frozone ducked as the claw whirled toward the Omnidroid.
As the claw ripped through the Omnidroid's tough metal, it collapsed.

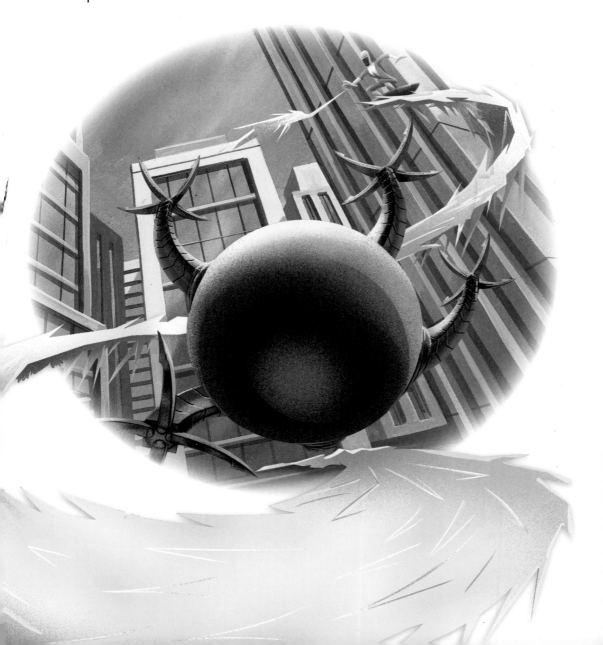

As the Omnidroid crashes through the streets of Municiburg, Lucius tries to imprison the metallic monster in icy handcuffs. But the raging robot easily breaks free. Then Lucius paves the street with ice so the Omnidroid slips and slides and isn't able to get a grip with its metal claws.

Cheering crowds poured into the street and surrounded Frozone and the Incredibles.

"Hey, 'Zone!" Bob said with a smile. "Just like the old times!" He slapped Frozone on the back so hard Frozone winced.

"Yeah, it hurt then, too," Frozone replied. But he was joking. He felt great! Using his super powers to stop the Omnidroid felt cool. Frozone grinned at his best pal. Even if he and Bob disagreed sometimes, they would always be a team. And for Frozone, that was the coolest thing of all.

Among the bystanders are two old gents who watch the battle with glee. "Did you see that? That's the way to do it! That's old school," they tell each other. They've been around long enough to know that when it comes to fighting evil, there's " no school like the old school."

JOKES, RIDDLES, AND SILLY STUFF!

... VOLUME 2 ANSWERS!

WHO DOES ELASTIGIRL
PLAY GUITAR WITH?
A RUBBER BAND.

WHY DID FROZONE
FREEZE HIS MONEY?
HE WANTED COLD,
HARD CASH.

WHAT CAN BABY
JACK-JACK HOLD
WITHOUT TOUCHING
ANYTHING?
HIS BREATH.

WHAT WAS THE
SOUND THAT WOKE
MR. INCREDIBLE UP
THIS MORNING?
THE CRACK OF DAWN!

WHY DOES FROZONE'S
FAMILY KEEP THE
BANDAGES IN THE
REFRIGERATOR?
FOR COLD CUTS.

WITHOUT HIS
SUPERHERO IDENTITY,
HOW DID
MR. INCREDIBLE
FIND A LOST BUNNY?
HE MADE NOISE
LIKE A CARROT.

WHY DID THE
OMNIDROID SNEEZE?
IT HAD A
COMPUTER VIRUS.

WHAT'S THE
INCREDIBLES'
FAVORITE SNACK?
A HERO SANDWICH.

WHERE SHOULD A
500 POUND
SUPERHERO GO?
ON A DIET.

WHICH SUPERHEROES
CAN FLY HIGHER THAN
A SKYSCRAPER?
ALL FLYING
SUPERHEROES—
BECAUSE SKYSCRAPERS
DON'T FLY.

UNSCRAMBLE THE
NAMES OF THE HERO
SYNDROME DESTROYED:
GAMEZEBRA: GAZERBEAM

WHAT DID ELASTIGIRL'S
LICENSE PLATE SAY?
X10DBL
(EXCITABLE)

WHAT'S THE NAME OF LUCIUS
BEST'S NEW YOGURT SHOP?
FRO YO ZONE.

WHY DID DASH RUN
AROUND THE BED?
TO CATCH UP ON HIS SLEEP.

WHAT IS ELASTIGIRL'S FAVORITE
PART OF BASEBALL?
THE SEVENTH INNING STRETCH.

WHICH IS FASTER,
HOT OR COLD?
HOT'S FASTER. YOU
CAN CATCH A COLD.

WHAT'S ANOTHER
NAME FOR ICE?
SKID STUFF!

IF TWO IS COMPANY AND
THREE'S A CROWD, WHAT'S
FOUR AND FIVE?
NINE.

ONE OF MR. INCREDIBLE'S
FAVORITE THINGS HAS NO
BEGINNING, NO MIDDLE
AND NO END. WHAT IS IT?
A DOUGHNUT.

WHY IS NOMANISAN
LIKE THE LETTER T?
IT'S IN THE MIDDLE OF WATER.

WHAT DID OMNIDROID
SAY TO GAZERBEAM?
LET'S GO KICK SOME ROBOT!

WHAT DOES EVEN A
SUPERHERO OVERLOOK?
HIS NOSE.

MR. INCREDIBLE:
I HAVE MADE A NEW INVENTION!
MRS. INCREDIBLE:
WHAT DOES IT DO?
MR. INCREDIBLE:
IT ALLOWS ORDINARY
PEOPLE TO SEE THROUGH
BRICK WALLS.
MRS. INCREDIBLE:
WHAT IS IT CALLED?
MR. INCREDIBLE:
IT'S CALLED A WINDOW!

MR. INCREDIBLE AND FROZONE
HAVE A KIND OF SHIP THAT NEVER
SINKS. WHAT IS IT CALLED?
FRIENDSHIP

WHAT IS THE BEST
MONTH FOR A PARADE TO
HONOR SUPERHEROES?
MARCH.

HOW COOL IS FROZONE?
HE'S SO COOL, HE MAKES
REFRIGERATORS REDUNDANT.

HOW DID SYNDROME KNOW WHEN
HE WAS NO LONGER WANTED?
THEY TOOK DOWN HIS PICTURE
AT THE POST OFFICE.

HOW FAST IS DASH?
HE'S SO FAST,
HE LAPPED HIMSELF!

HOW STRONG IS MR. INCREDIBLE?
HE'S SO STRONG, WHEN HE
DOES PUSH-UPS, HE'S ACTUALLY
PUSHING THE WORLD DOWN!